LiTtLE CRiTtER'S®
STAYING
OVERNIGHT

BY
MERCER MAYER

To Arden,
The New Little Mayer

A Golden Book • New York
Western Publishing Company, Inc., Racine, Wisconsin 53404

I am going to sleep
at my friend's house.
His house is big.

Someone in funny clothes
opened the door.
There was my friend!

I said good-bye
to Mom.

Time to play!

We went
into the pool.

We played games
with balls.

We played tag.
We had a race.

We played
hide-and-seek.

Then we played
more games with balls.

Then we went inside.
My friend has
all of the
Bozo Builder Set.

He has a train
with lots of things.

His bear is big—
bigger than my bear.

But his dog
is small.
His dog is named
Froo-Froo.

It was time for dinner.
The napkin looked
like a hat.
I put it
on my head.

My friend has a TV
in his room.
We watched until
it was late.

It was time for bed.

We turned out
the lights.
It was dark—
a bigger dark
than in my room.

So I hugged my bear.

The next day
we played outside
again.

No, Froo-Froo!
Come back!

Stop, Froo-Froo!
Stop! Stop!

Got you!

It was a good time
to call Mom.

Thank you
for everything.
Bye-bye!

I had fun
at my friend's house.
But home is best.